D1380480

For Esme and Henry and for Jess, my super supportive mum – S.C.
For Max and Matthew – G.M.

First published in 2020 by Nosy Crow Ltd
The Crow's Nest, 14 Baden Place
Crosby Row, London, SE1 1YW
www.nosycrow.com

ISBN 978 1 78800 768 9 (HB) • ISBN 978 1 78800 769 6 (PB)
Nosy Crow and associated logos are trademarks
and/or registered trademarks of Nosy Crow Ltd.

Text copyright © Stephanie Clarkson 2020 • Illustrations copyright © Gwen Millward 2020
The right of Stephanie Clarkson to be identified as the author and of
Gwen Millward to be identified as the illustrator of this work has been asserted.

All rights reserved

This book is sold subject to the condition that it shall not,
by way of trade or otherwise, be lent, hired out or otherwise circulated in any
form of binding or cover other than that in which it is published. No part of this publication
may be reproduced, stored in a retrieval system, or transmitted in any form or by any means
(electronic, mechanical, photocopying, recording or otherwise)
without the prior written permission of Nosy Crow Ltd.

A CIP catalogue record for this book is available from the British Library.

Printed in China
Papers used by Nosy Crow are made from wood grown in sustainable forests.

1 2 3 4 5 6 7 8 9 10 (HB)
1 2 3 4 5 6 7 8 9 10 (PB)

Super Milly and the Super School Day

STEPHANIE CLARKSON
GWEN MILLWARD

nosy crow

I am SUPER MILLY!
M

Today is **Superhero Day** at school.

I have used all the tinfoil,
a tea towel with only one hole
– which doesn't even show –
a pair of my brother Joe's pants,
and a **big badge** with an **M**.

But . . .

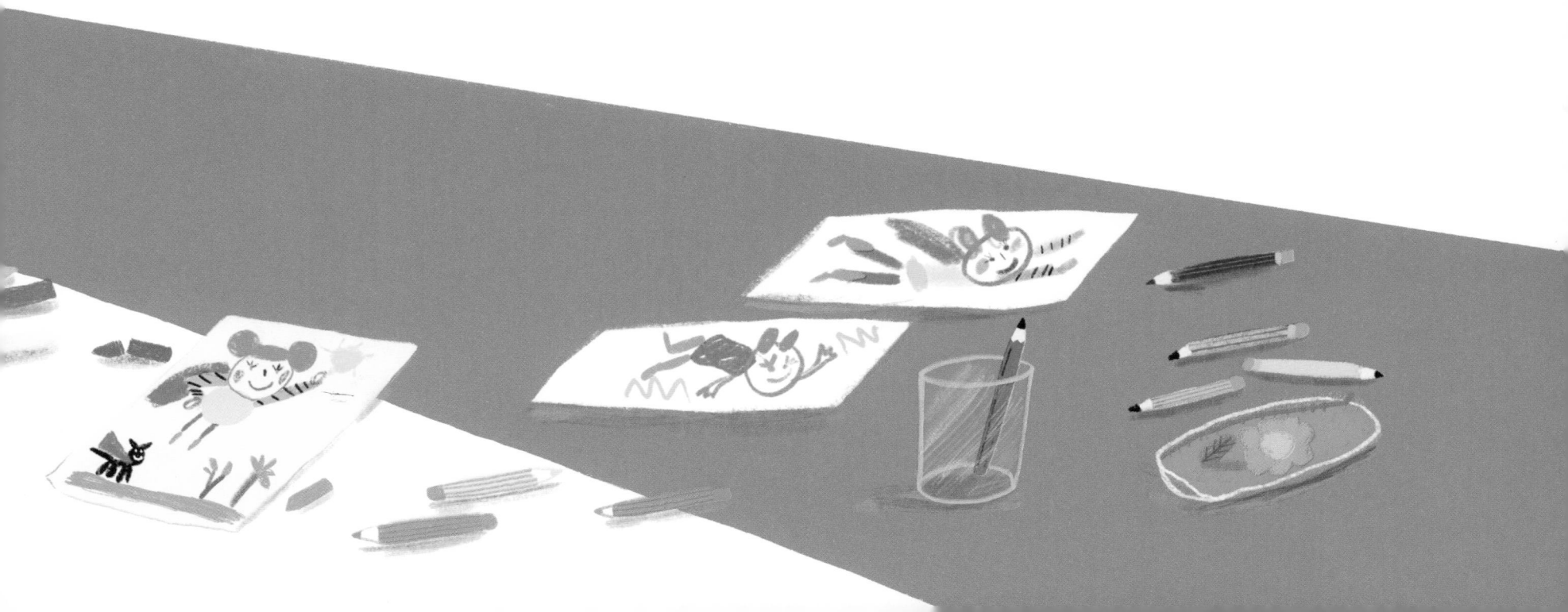

. . . I don't have
X-ray vision . . .

I can't **climb**
up buildings . . .

and **superheroes** are supposed to
beat the baddies . . .

but I can't stop Joe taking
the last bit of toast.

I don't have **any** special powers.

When I get into class, there is already a big **emergency**.

William's dad has forgotten that it is Superhero Day. William is crying in the book corner . . . in his normal trousers!

A **real superhero**
would spin around
William **super fast . . .**

until his outfit changed.

But Miss Kent says, "Bottoms
on seats please, Milly."

So, I think hard and . . .

. . . I unpin my special badge.

"You can be **Wonder William**," I say.
"But it's an **M**," he says.
I pin it on him upside down.
"Now it's a **W**!"

BAM!

Wonder William says
I am **super** kind.

Next, we have to write about
"A Day in the Life of a **Superhero**".

Fantastic Flora is not keen on writing.

Her **b**s keep looking like **d**s.

A **real superhero** would use
mega mind power . . .

to make Flora's pencil
write all by itself!

But the pencil stays still.
William says it moved, but
that's because he pushed it
a bit with his finger.

I think really hard and . . .

. . . "Hey, Flora!" I say. "What has a cape and goes round and round?

A superhero in a washing machine."

Fantastic Flora says I am **super** funny and writes down the joke all by herself.

In the afternoon, we do art.

Amazing Archie wants to paint a supervillain,
but **Spider Sid** is hogging the green paint.

A **real superhero**
would grab the green . . .

and fly at **super speed**
between Archie and Sid,
so that they can share.

But my flying cape
is trapped under
my apron!

I think really,
really hard and . . .

. . . "We can mix blue and yellow together to make green!" I say.
ZAP!
Amazing Archie is amazed and says I am **super** clever!

He loves green so much he paints **everything** – including William!

It is nearly home time.

Incredible Iqbal has brought in a minibeast for Show and Tell. Spider Sid says it is really rubbish and not even a tarantula. Iqbal's voice goes all quiet . . .

and then the spider escapes!

There is a **lot** of screaming . . .

. . . until Fantastic Flora
catches it again.

But Spider Sid is laughing
and pointing at me and Iqbal.

A **real superhero** would
make a **force field** around us,
so no one can hurt our feelings.

But it's hard to do force fields when you are turning as red as a tomato.

I do some supersonic thinking and . . .

. . . have a brilliant idea!
I hold hands with Iqbal, and our
superness gets stronger . . .

Then, in my **loudest** voice, I tell the class
that spiders have blue blood and can spin
silk. Iqbal's voice comes back, and he spells
out the name for the fear of spiders –

"A R A C H N O P H O B I A."

WHIZZ!
Incredible Iqbal says
I am **super** brave.
WHAM!
Everyone claps and says
I am a **super** good friend.
Spider Sid does a
really loud cheer.

I am **SUPER MILLY!**
Maybe I **do** have special powers after all . . .

BAM!
I am kind.

KABOOM!
I am funny.

ZAP!
I am clever.

WHIZZ!
I am brave.

WHAM!
I am a good friend.

These are **my** superpowers!

KERPOW!
I bet **you** have superpowers too.